S0-BSD-764

Bill Cosby's Little Bill

Shipwreck Saturday

Bill Cosby's
Little Bill

GROWING READER
LEVEL 3
700-1500 WORDS

Shipwreck Saturday

by Bill Cosby
Illustrated by Varnette P. Honeywood

Cartwheel
·B·O·O·K·S·®

SCHOLASTIC INC.
New York Toronto London Auckland Sydney
Mexico City New Delhi Hong Kong Buenos Aires

No part of this publication may be reproduced, stored in a retrieval system, or transmitted in any form or by any means, electronic, mechanical, photocopying, recording, or otherwise, without written permission of the publisher. For information regarding permission, write to Scholastic Inc., Attention: Permissions Department, 557 Broadway, New York, NY 10012.

Copyright © 1998 by Bill Cosby.

All rights reserved. Published by Scholastic Inc.
SCHOLASTIC, CARTWHEEL BOOKS, and associated logos
are trademarks and/or registered trademarks of Scholastic Inc.
LITTLE BILL is a trademark of Bill Cosby.
Lexile is a registered trademark of MetaMetrics, Inc.

Library of Congress Cataloging-in-Publication Data is available.

ISBN-13: 978-0-590-95620-8
ISBN-10: 0-590-95620-5

28 27 26 25   09 10 11 12/0

Printed in the U.S.A. 23 • This edition first printing, April 2008

To Ennis,
"Hello, friend,"
B.C.

To the Cosby Family,
Ennis's perseverance against the odds
is an inspiration to us all,
V.P.H.

Dear Parent:

Not many years ago, children used to make at least some of their own toys, either building models from kits or applying their imagination to materials they found around the house or on the street. Many children, of course, dreamed of having more store-bought toys even though it was fun to make their own. Now, a dream-come-true array of manufactured toys has replaced most do-it-yourself efforts.

Progress? Not entirely. Relying on ready-made toys restricts children to someone else's ideas about play, but spending time and effort on building home-made toys helps children develop in valuable ways. They strengthen their imagination, patience, and perseverance; improve their manual dexterity; and (with a kit) sharpen their ability to follow directions. Best of all, they experience the satisfaction that comes from producing something, start to finish, with one's own hands.

Children often feel a deep attachment to a toy they've made themselves, and we see this in *Shipwreck Saturday*. Little Bill takes immense pride in a toy sailboat he has built. And when the boat is wrecked, his shock and grief cause him to leave his friends abruptly and run home to cry. It would be hard to imagine our cool hero reacting that way to losing a boat he picked up at the toy store.

Besides giving your child an example of how much fun it is to make a toy, this story shows how creativity can transform a painful experience. After Little Bill runs off, his friend Kiku salvages the mast of his ruined boat to make a beautiful kite. When Bill returns to face his loss, he finds her flying the new kite before an admiring crowd. Kiku considerately hands the kite string over to him, and Little Bill's grief is gone with the wind.

Alvin F. Poussaint, M.D.
Clinical Professor of Psychiatry,
Harvard Medical School and
Judge Baker Children's Center,
Boston, MA

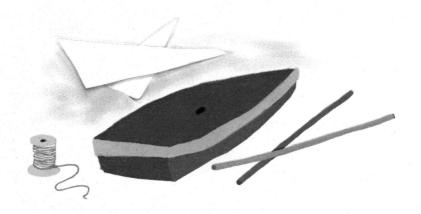

Chapter 1

Hi! I'm Little Bill. This is a story about a boat that I made all by myself. I named it *The Moby Dick*.

One Saturday morning, I woke up and saw that it was bright and sunny outside. Hurray! I could go with my brother to the park and sail my new boat.

I quickly got dressed and put on my baseball cap. First I put it on the right way. Then I put it on backward. I tried the brim on the side. Then I put it on forward again and pushed the brim down low. It looked very cool.

Running to the kitchen, I bumped into my dad.

"Slow down," he said.

Mom pulled up the brim of my cap. "You can't see a thing," she said.

I pushed it back down.

Mom pushed it up again.

Bobby and I ate breakfast while Mom packed a lunch for each of us— peanut butter and jelly on whole wheat bread, a banana, and a juice box.

"I'm going to try out the boat I made
last week," I said.

I finished breakfast first and pulled
Bobby away from the table.

"Be back by four o'clock," Mom said.

I grabbed my lunch, kissed Mom, high-fived Dad, and ran out the door behind Bobby.

Oops! I almost forgot my boat.

I ran back to my room and carefully took the boat off the shelf. I couldn't wait to test it out and show it off. I ran back outside to meet Bobby.

Chapter 2

Bobby's friends were waiting at the corner. We started to walk toward the park. "Hey, Little Bill. Did you make that boat?" Matt asked.

"Yes," I said proudly.

"You don't think it will sail, do you?" asked Brian.

I nodded. "Yes, I do."

"It will sail all right," said Matt, "right to the bottom of the lake."

That made me mad.
I worked hard to make my
boat. And I was going to sail it!
I started to run as I got closer to the
lake.
"I'll be at the courts," Bobby yelled.
"I'll check on you later."

I looked at the benches around the lake, and I saw a girl with a rainbow ribbon in her hair. It was my friend, Kiku, and she was with her grandmother.

"This is *origami*," Kiku's grandmother said, "the Japanese art of paper folding. You can make many things. Like a swan, a flower, and a fan."

Girl things, I thought.

"And boats," said Kiku's grandmother.

I showed them the boat that I had made. "The sails are paper. The rest is wood," I said.

"Cool," said Kiku.

We walked to the lake. I carefully placed *The Moby Dick* in the water. The breeze caught its sails and it floated away.

Kiku warned me not to let it go out too far. But I had a long roll of string. I let the string out more and more until *The Moby Dick* was in the middle of the lake.

Suddenly, a rowboat came by. SWISH! The ripples in the lake grew into waves. SPLASH! A wave rolled over my boat. And SMASH! went my boat into the other boat.

Kiku told me to rewind the string, but I was too shocked to move. Kiku took the string from my hand and pulled the boat in for me.

Her grandmother came over to us with two paper boats. But I didn't want to sail a paper boat. My boat was ruined. The mast was broken. The sails were soaked.

I didn't want Kiku to see me cry, so I ran home without my boat, without my lunch, and without my brother.

Chapter 3

At home, I threw myself on my bed and cried.

Dad came into my room. "What happened? Where's your brother? Where's your boat?"

I told Dad what happened. "You shouldn't have left the park without Bobby," he said.

I knew my dad was right. "I'm sorry," I said.

"Let's go to the park and see what we can do," said Dad.

I didn't want to go. Bobby and his friends would laugh at me. Kiku would laugh at me, too. "Do I have to go?"

My father nodded, "I think it would be best. Besides, I'll be with you."

At the park, I saw a crowd with Bobby and his friends, Kiku and her grandmother. I wanted to hide, so I pulled my baseball cap down over my face. I didn't feel cool anymore.

"Look," said Dad. He pulled the cap off my face.

Everyone was looking up at a beautiful kite that flew over the lake. The tail was made from Kiku's ribbon, and the frame, Kiku told me, was made from the sticks from my boat.

Kiku gave me the roll of string.

"That's a great kite," Bobby said.

"It's my boat," I said. "What's left of it."

"Cool, man," said Bobby.

Everyone laughed. And that was
okay with me.

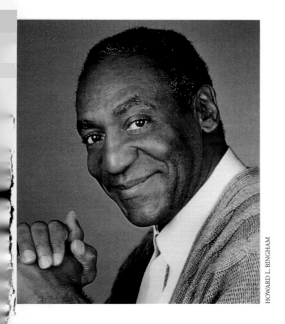

Bill Cosby is one of America's best-loved storytellers, known for his work as a comedian, actor, and producer. His books for adults include *Fatherhood*, *Time Flies*, *Love and Marriage*, and *Childhood*. Mr. Cosby holds a doctoral degree in education from the University of Massachusetts.

Varnette P. Honeywood, a graduate of Spelman College and the University of Southern California, is a Los Angeles-based fine artist. Her work is included in many collections throughout the United States and Africa and has appeared on adult trade book jackets and in other books in the Little Bill series.

Books in the LITTLE BILL series: